To Sheila Perry,
who first introduced me to
the glories of Venice

SIMON AND SCHUSTER
First published in Great Britain in 2010 by Simon and Schuster UK Ltd
1st Floor, 222 Gray's Inn Road, London, WC1X 8HB
A CBS Company

Originally published in 2010 by Atheneum Books for Young Readers,
an imprint of Simon and Schuster Children's Publishing Division, New York

Book design by Ann Bobco
The text for this book is set in Centaur.
The illustrations for this book are rendered in charcoal and gouache on paper, combined with photographs digitally altered in Photoshop.

A CIP catalogue record for this book is available from the British Library upon request

ISBN: 978 1 84738 835 3

Printed in China

10 9 8 7 6 5 4 3 2 1

OLIVIA

goes to

Venice

written and illustrated by   Ian Falconer

SIMON AND SCHUSTER
LONDON   NEW YORK   SYDNEY   TORONTO

It was time for spring vacation. Olivia decided that she and her family ought to spend a few days in Venice. There was a lot of packing to be done.

"Olivia, you won't be needing your snorkel," said her mother, "or your flippers."

"Mother, apparently the city is often under water and — "

"Or your water skis."

As they went through the airport, Olivia was searched for weapons. She was very pleased.

On the plane Olivia asked her mother about the food in Venice.

"Don't worry, sweetheart, you can get pizza and ice cream everywhere."

"EVERYWHERE?!"

Olivia was relieved.

They arrived very late at their hotel. Olivia was so sleepy, she didn't even notice the view from her window.

Early the next morning
they set forth.
They crossed a pretty
little bridge.
And then another.
And then another.

"Wait!"
cried Olivia.

"We've been crossing the same canal!
I think we're lost. And my blood sugar
is getting low."

"We'll get some ice cream,"
promised her mother.

"It's called gelato,"
replied Olivia.

They all decided to have gelato.

Crossing a big bridge, Olivia saw the Grand Canal for the
first time, lined with its glittering many-coloured palazzos.

Olivia said to her mother with an edge
of hysteria in her voice, "Oh, please –
OH, PLEASE, MOTHER –
can't we live in a palazzo
on the Grand Canal?"

It was a life-changing experience for Olivia.
She needed another gelato.

Or maybe two . . .

. . . or three.

When she was refreshed,
they wandered on.

Finally, they passed
through a dark archway . . .

. . . and into the Piazza San Marco.
Olivia was overcome by its beauty. "Mother,
I think I could use another — "

Her mother sighed. "I think we all could."

Olivia wanted to buy corn
to feed the pigeons.

She held out the corn, but couldn't find many pigeons.

But they soon found her.

After that exhausting encounter
Olivia required another gelato.

GONDOLA!
GONDOLA!

The next day Olivia begged
her parents, "Oh, Mummy,
Daddy – PLEASE can we take
a gondola ride?"

Olivia negotiated the price. The gondolier waved
them aboard with a gallant *"Prego."*

Olivia found it very restful.
The gondolier did not.

They came out onto the Grand Canal and passed under the magnificent Rialto Bridge.

Eventually they emerged
out from under the
Bridge of Sighs.

Olivia sighed.

By now, Olivia was
completely entranced.
"I must have something
to remember Venice by.
I must find the perfect
souvenir.

"How about a chandelier?"

"Olivia, that's bigger than your
room!" said her mother.

"What about a gondola?"

"Sweetheart, try to find something you can carry."

Lace?

Very pretty, but not really very Olivia.

A mask?

No, thought Olivia, *I'll only wear it once.*

Perfume?

Olivia doesn't really like perfume.

Besides, she's planning her own line.

On their last day in Venice, Olivia and her family went back
to San Marco.

The basilica was all peach and gold in the late afternoon light. Mother and Father were finishing their coffee. Olivia and Ian were playing by the bell tower.

"I found it!" cried Olivia. "The perfect souvenir!"
"What is that?" asked her mother.
"One of the actual Stones of Venice," said Olivia.
"From the bell tower."

"OLIVIA!" said her mother.
"If everyone took a piece of Venice
with them, the city would fall down.
Now leave that with the waiter.
We've got to get to the airport."

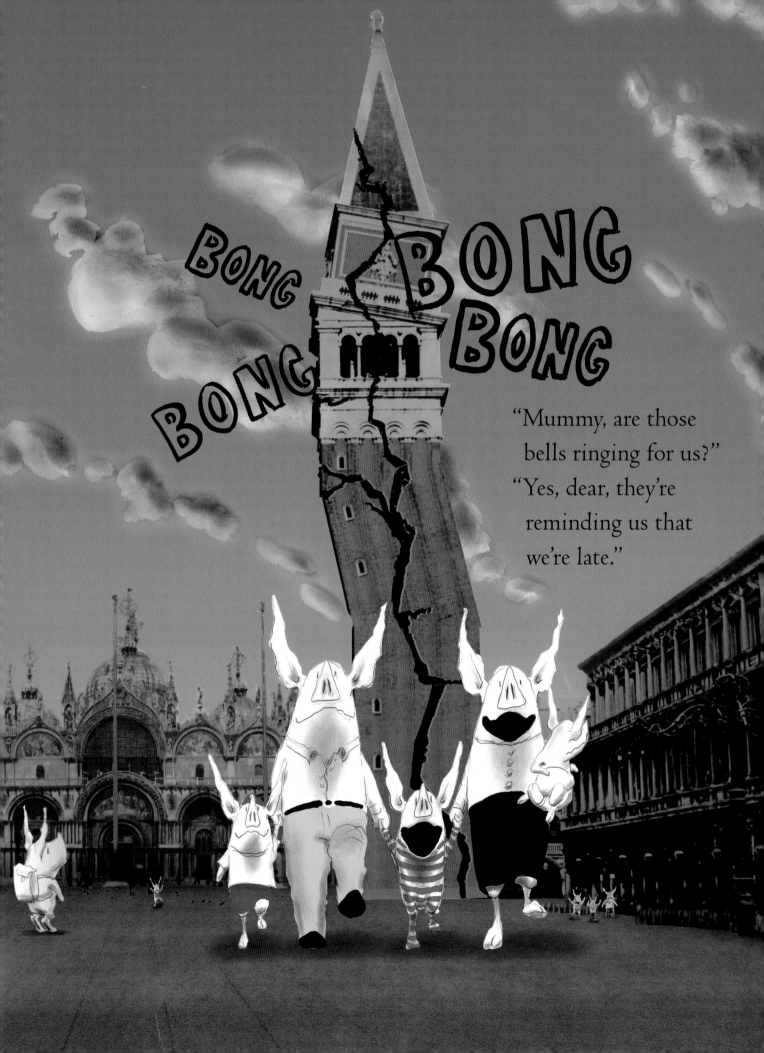

Olivia turned to take one last look at Venice.

"Look, they're waving us goodbye. . .

I'll always remember Venice,
Mummy. Do you think
Venice will remember me?"

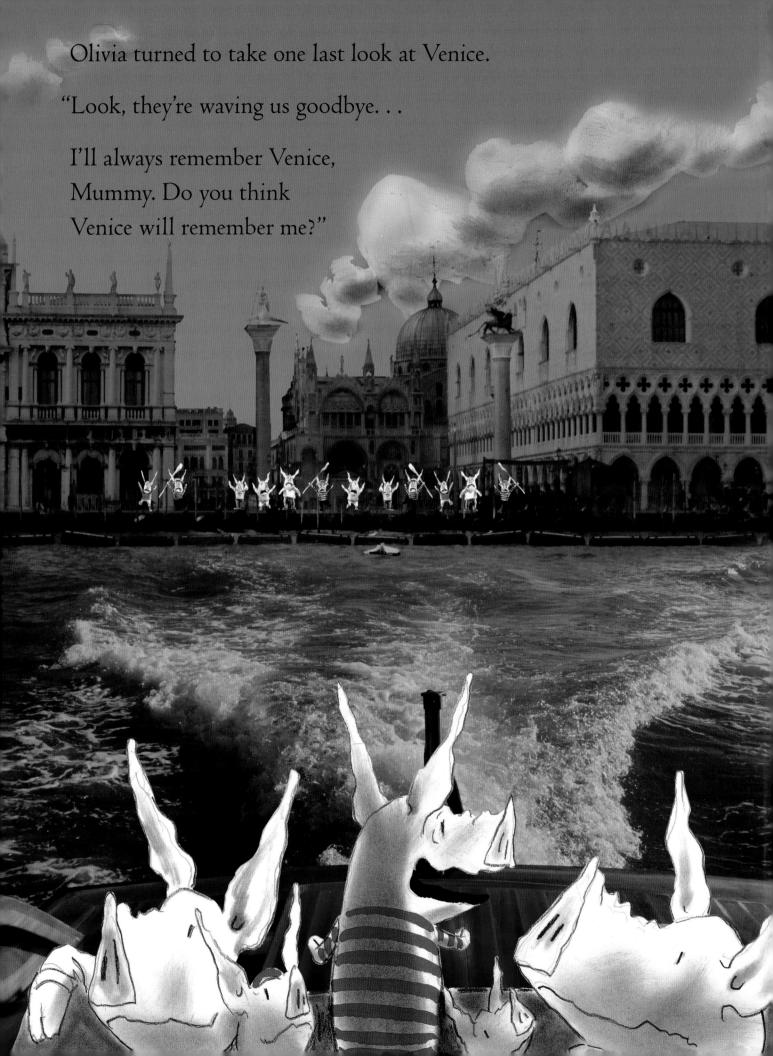

"Probably."

As soon as she got on the plane, Olivia fell fast asleep . . .

MONUMENTO
OLIVIA
←

. . . and dreamed.